THE
LOST
BEAR CUB

For Caroline
HW

For Mum and Dad
DD

LITTLE TIGER
An imprint of Little Tiger Press Limited
1 Coda Studios, 189 Munster Road,
London SW6 6AW

Imported into the EEA by Penguin Random House Ireland,
Morrison Chambers, 32 Nassau Street, Dublin D02 YH68

www.littletiger.co.uk

A paperback original
First published in Great Britain in 2023

ISBN: 978-1-78895-606-2

A CIP catalogue record for this book is available
from the British Library.

Printed and bound in the UK.

The Forest Stewardship Council® (FSC®) is a global, not-for-profit organization
dedicated to the promotion of responsible forest management worldwide. FSC®
defines standards based on agreed principles for responsible forest stewardship
that are supported by environmental, social, and economic stakeholders.
To learn more, visit www.fsc.org

2 4 6 8 10 9 7 5 3 1

THE
LOST
BEAR CUB

Holly Webb
Illustrated by David Dean

LiTTLE TiGER

LONDON

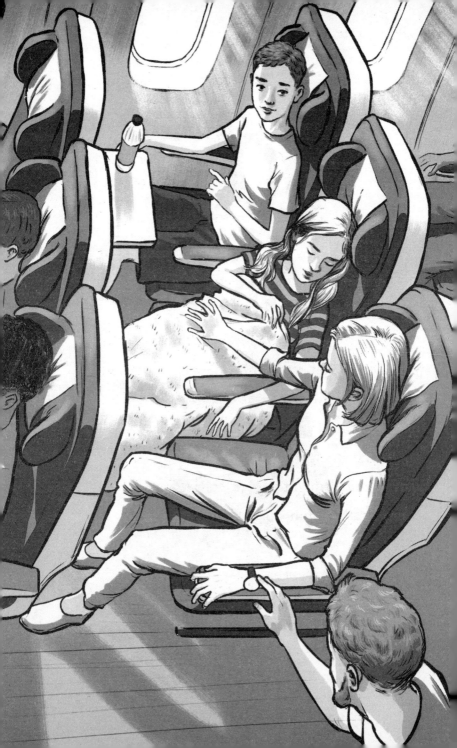

"Lucy…Wake up, sweetheart. We're nearly there. Hey… Lucy…"

Lucy blinked and snuggled further into the fleecy blanket Mum had wrapped around her. She'd spent ages trying to get to sleep on the plane but it had all been too different and strange. She'd even enjoyed the aeroplane food. It might not have tasted very nice but it had been fun, opening all the little boxes and packets.

"I've only been asleep a minute," she murmured, blinking around at the bright cabin. There was an energy in the air now – people were folding their blankets away and searching through the seat pockets. A garbled announcement came over the speaker.

"We'll be landing soon," her mum explained. "You need to put your seat belt on. Can you feel the plane going down?"

Lucy frowned as she fiddled with the fastening of her seat belt, wondering how she would know. She'd never been on a plane before – but actually, her ears felt strange. Was that it? "I think my ears are popping."

"I've got some mints you can suck, that'll help."

Dad leaned over, smiling at her. He looked so excited, Lucy thought. He'd been like that for months. Ever since they'd started to plan their trip to Canada. Dad's only brother, Lucy's uncle Pete, had gone to live in Canada years before. Lucy had never met him, and though they all said hello to each other on video calls – Lucy and her big brother Jack and their uncle's children too – it wasn't the same as really knowing someone.

Now they were going to stay for a whole month of the summer holidays at Uncle Pete and Auntie Cass's house. There were two older boy cousins, Reuben and Sam, and Kitty who was about six months older than Lucy. Lucy was as excited as Dad but she was nervous too. What if they didn't get on with their cousins? Just because they were family didn't mean they were actually going to *like* each other. Lucy loved spending time with her friends at school but she didn't think she was very good at meeting new people. She never knew what to say. Mum, Dad and Lucy's friends from school who'd known her for ages said she was really funny but someone she'd just met wouldn't know it.

Lucy had two other cousins back in England, Georgie and Marcus, but they were younger than she was. They loved her and Jack because they were big and grown up. Now Lucy was going to be the youngest and the quietest... What if she spent the summer holidays hardly talking at all?

Lucy unwrapped the mint her dad had given her and slipped it into her mouth. She wasn't going to worry about all that now. Dad had kept saying it was going to be an adventure – they were going to camp out, and there would be all this amazing wildlife to see. Uncle Pete had sent them photos of moose walking down

the street near where he lived, and even a bear
sunbathing in a neighbour's garden.

"Look!" Jack nudged her and pointed out of
the window, and Lucy leaned over to see past
her brother.

"Wow," she whispered,
peering down
through the clouds.
"Mountains! They
look so big. Is that
snow on the top?"
It had been really
sunny and hot
back at home, so
it felt odd to see
patches of snow
snaking down the
rocky crags.

"They're very tall, so they probably have a bit of snow all year round," Dad said, craning over from his seat on the other side of the aisle. "Not long now!"

Lucy threaded her hand with Mum's as they both stared out of the window. Her ears felt very odd, as though someone was pressing their hands around the sides of her head, but the view outside was so amazing that she could almost ignore it.

"Look at that lake!" Jack pointed again. Lucy leaned as far as she could and spotted the jewel-bright blue water against the dark mountains.

"It's beautiful," she murmured. It all looked so different too, wild and strange and magical. Lucy's nervousness was still there a little but the excitement was taking over. There was a city of skyscrapers below them now, with the mountains rising up behind and the sea stretching round. Lucy had never seen anything like it before – she couldn't wait to land.

An hour later, all the sleep Lucy hadn't had on the plane was catching up with her. She tried to swallow a yawn and the airport official checking their passports smiled. "You can't be tired now. I bet you've got a full day ahead of you."

Lucy nodded shyly, loving the Canadian accent.

"You're all done. Welcome to Vancouver!"

"Thank you!" Mum put her arm round Lucy and scooted them forwards. "We need to head for baggage reclaim and get our suitcases," she explained to Jack and Lucy.

"And I can send a message to Pete, telling

him we're nearly ready for him to pick us up,"
Dad said. "Their house is about a forty-five-
minute drive away." He looked round at the
bustling airport and shook his head. "Hard to
believe, isn't it – there's the busy city and then
the wild mountains, and they're practically next
to each other!"

It took longer than Lucy could have believed
to get their luggage – they seemed to be
watching the same suitcases that weren't theirs
go round the carousel for ages – but at last they
appeared and they grabbed them then headed
through the airport to meet Uncle Pete.

Lucy hadn't realized how much he'd look like
Dad when they saw him for real, standing by
the barrier and waving. In photos and on video
calls he and Dad didn't seem alike at all but
it was something about the way they stood.

It made her like Uncle Pete at once.

"I wish I could have brought everybody," he said, taking one of the big suitcases after he'd given them a hug. "The whole family wanted to come to greet you. But we wouldn't have all been able to fit in the car. I've sorted out hiring one for you while you're here."

Lucy trotted along after them, wheeling her bag and trying not to bump into people. She stifled another yawn, wishing she'd slept more on the plane. She didn't want to miss any of their first view of Canada.

Mum sat in the middle of the back seat so Lucy and Jack could be by the windows. The airport was on an island but once they'd got over the bridges to the mainland, the first part of the journey looked a lot like their drive to the airport back home. Lots of shops and houses – and cars.

THE LOST BEAR CUB

Until they came out of the edges of the
city and started to see flashes of startlingly
blue water between the dark pine trees, and
mountains on the other side of the water. It all
looked wild and exciting, even from inside a car.

"Those are more islands over there," Uncle Pete called from the front seat. "You're seeing it on a good day, it's beautiful with the sun on the water."

y whispered, as a break in the
d them the ruffled surface of the
wat... ipples glinting in the sun.

Uncle Pete laughed. "That's how I felt when
I first saw it, Lucy. It's the most beautiful
place to live. Here." He rustled about in
the pocket of the car door and passed back
a handful of leaflets. "Here, you two, take a
look at these – some of the amazing places
we're going to take you to."

Lucy and Jack flicked through them,
looking at hiking trails, a kayaking centre
and camping grounds. "Mum, look…"
Lucy whispered, holding up a leaflet about
a campsite. Across the top, in big black
capitals, it said:

THIS IS
BEAR COUNTRY

"Same here," Jack said, pointing at another one.

"What's that?" Dad said, turning round in his seat. "Wow, bears, they don't want you to miss that, do they?"

Uncle Pete snorted. "No, they do not. We have to be so careful round here. Often people get themselves into trouble because they don't take it seriously; they think the bears are cute. Mind you, I think moose are more dangerous than bears." He slowed the car, shaking his head. "Uh-oh, I shouldn't have said anything. Hey, you two, look out the front."

"Is that a moose?" Jack yelped.

"Two. A mother and a calf." Uncle Pete sounded quite proud, as though he'd laid on the moose specially. "You see them quite often along here. We have to watch out when we're driving. Mostly it's deer on the roads but you get moose too, and sometimes a bear…"

The moose were just strolling across the road, as though they hadn't a care in the world. They didn't seem bothered about the cars – perhaps they knew that everyone would stop for them. The mother was huge, definitely taller than Dad, Lucy thought.

She had a long, blunt nose, a bit like a camel, and such spindly legs. Her baby padded behind her, looking tiny next to its huge mother.

"Such big ears," Mum said, watching as the two moose disappeared into the trees. "But no horns?"

"Only the bull moose have those," Uncle Pete explained. "They're usually a lot bigger as well."

"Even bigger than that…" Lucy murmured. "How old was that baby one, Uncle Pete?"

"I think they're usually born at the beginning of summer," her uncle said thoughtfully. "Around June? So maybe a couple of months old. Definitely a lucky spot on your first day. We'll have to see what else we can find to top that!"

"They're here!"

Lucy could hear someone shouting excitedly even before Uncle Pete stopped the car and then what seemed like a huge number of people spilled out of the house to meet them. Dad opened Lucy's door and she climbed out slowly, looking at her cousins. Luckily Reuben was a lot taller than Sam so it was easy to tell them apart. She was just noticing that he had darker

hair too, when someone suddenly hugged
her and she squeaked. Her cousin Kitty
had run round the side of the car without
Lucy realizing.

"Hey, Lucy! I'm Kitty, your cousin. Did you have a good journey? Did you like the plane? Were you airsick? I get sick whenever I'm in a plane. And cars sometimes."

"Hi…" Lucy gazed at her, a bit daunted by the flood of words – but at least her cousin seemed friendly. Kitty was smaller than she was, Lucy realized, feeling a bit pleased. She was the youngest child there but at least she wasn't the smallest.

"Wow, you're really tall." Kitty stepped back and eyed her, looking a bit surprised. "I thought I'd be taller than you since I'm older. I'm ten."

"I'm ten in September," Lucy told her. It wasn't that long.

"You're staying in my room – I've got a bed that pulls out from underneath mine. Want me to help carry your stuff?"

"Um, thanks." Lucy handed Kitty her little backpack and walked round to the back of the car to grab her suitcase. Her cousin seemed really friendly, which was good. And it would be fun sharing a room – she'd never done that before, except on a few sleepovers with friends from school.

"Everyone got all their stuff?" Uncle Pete asked, peering into the back of the car. "No one left any snacks or anything in the seat pockets?" He grinned at Kitty as he said it but it sounded like he was serious. Lucy shook her head uncertainly. Was he worried about things getting left in the car and going off? Mum had got really annoyed with Jack once for leaving an apple core in the car door where it started to grow horrible grey furry mildew.

"I don't think Jack or Lucy had any snacks…"

Mum said – she sounded uncertain too.

"It's not that I'm fussy about the car," Uncle Pete explained. "You know I said we have to be careful about bears. I really meant it. If you leave food in the car they can break in looking for it. It's not a problem if it's in the trunk and well covered up, but wrappers and stuff in the back, that's just asking for trouble."

Jack and Kitty exchanged a glance. Was Uncle Pete having them on?

"Hang on, how would bears know about the food?" Dad asked, looking puzzled.

"They've got the most amazing sense of smell," Uncle Pete said. "And believe it or not, they can open car doors, even if they're locked. Car doors don't stand up to five centimetres of claws, not when a bear wants in. It's absolutely true, Martin, I promise. It actually happened

to me not long after I moved out here. I parked
up the car close to a trail and went hiking,
and I'd left some supplies on the back seat.
I locked the car, but it was an old model and
the bear didn't have much trouble getting in.
It ate all the food and ripped the seats to
shreds in case I was hiding anything else."
Uncle Pete shrugged. "Now I always check.
A bear might have more of a problem with
a newer car, but it's not worth the risk."

"Dad! You never told us that!" Reuben shook
his head, laughing.

"It's not just food either," Auntie Cass put in.
"Anything with a strong, sweet sort of smell,
like a packet of wet wipes."

Mum looked worriedly at their bags, and
Lucy knew she was thinking that she usually
had wet wipes in her handbag, just in case.

"I don't think you got them out in the car," she whispered, and Mum smiled.

"I think we've got a lot to learn while we're here," she whispered back. "You definitely didn't have any biscuits or anything from the flight that you left in there? It would be awful if a bear ruined Uncle Pete's car..."

Lucy shuddered. Mum was right – that would *not* be a good start to the holiday.

Lucy woke late the next morning. She and
Kitty had found it difficult to get to sleep the
night before – Kitty had never shared her
bedroom either and it was just so hard to stop
talking. And talking. About what school was
like in Canada and how it was different from
back home, and all their friends, and what TV
programmes they watched, and games and
books and music... Between that and the time
difference, Lucy was so confused. And in the
end she wasn't sure if she'd gone to bed early
or late.

The pair of them trailed sleepily out into the main room of the house – which was a kitchen and living room all in one – drawn by a delicious sweet-savoury scent that Lucy couldn't pin down.

"I thought that might get you out of bed," Auntie Cass said to Kitty, smiling. "Hi, Lucy! Did you sleep well? I'm making something really Canadian for breakfast on your first day."

"Pancakes," Kitty said, perking up. "You'll love them, Lucy. They're my favourite thing."

Lucy watched Auntie Cass and Reuben spooning pancake batter into a big cast-iron pan. She loved pancakes back home but these looked different to the ones Mum made with lemon and sugar – they were small and fat and fluffy.

They smelled *amazing*.

"Sit down," Kitty told her, patting the stool next to her at the big kitchen island, and the family's grey cat Shadow leaped up on to the stool on Lucy's other side. She was sniffing hopefully at the breakfast too and Lucy stroked her ears. Their cat Billy had gone to stay with Gran while they were away. Lucy hoped he was OK. Gran was probably spoiling him.

Auntie Cass put a plate of pancakes in front of each of them. The pancakes were stacked in a little pile and there was crispy bacon on top. Lucy blinked. She'd never had bacon on pancakes before – and then Kitty handed her a bottle of maple syrup, which she'd just drizzled all over her plate.

Reuben laughed at her. "You look so worried. Don't you have pancakes at home?"

"Yes…" Lucy agreed shyly. "But not like this."

THE LOST BEAR CUB

"Try them," Auntie Cass said encouragingly. "But don't worry, Lucy. If you don't like them, Kitty will definitely eat them for you…"

Kitty stared at her hopefully, and Lucy poured on the syrup and took a mouthful. She was expecting it to be weird – bacon and sweet syrup? – but the flavours all mixed together and it was so good.

She smiled at Kitty, syrup smudging her lips. "Sorry, but these are mine."

Lucy's mum and dad and Jack were still sleeping, Auntie Cass explained. The jet lag had worn them out. But Auntie Cass and Uncle Pete had planned for a lazy morning, and then a walk along a nearby forest trail in the afternoon.

"Does that sound good, Lucy?" Auntie Cass asked, when she didn't say anything.

Lucy looked back at her. "Yes – sorry! Auntie Cass, look!"

Darting along the deck outside the living room were two cat-sized creatures – they

THE LOST BEAR CUB

looked like a cross between cats and monkeys, with dark pointed ears, black mask markings around their eyes, and long, dark stripey tails. One of them was sniffing about the floor of the deck, and the other one was scurrying along the rail at the edge, tail swinging.

"Are they raccoons?" Lucy asked, wide-eyed. Dad had told her to expect bears and moose, but no one had mentioned raccoons. They looked so funny – like little cartoon burglars in their masks.

Auntie Cass nodded. "Cute, aren't they? I swear those two can smell pancakes as well, just look at them."

The raccoon who'd been walking along the deck was now standing up with its narrow little front paws pressed against the glass doors, peering in. It really looked like it wanted pancakes.

"Are they tame?" Lucy asked, imagining – just perhaps – a raccoon sitting on her lap.

"Not at all," Auntie Cass said. "They can actually give you a nasty bite. Don't try and go near them. They're really fun to watch, though."

"They once stole my sneakers," Reuben growled, pretend-fierce. He pointed the spoon he'd been using for the pancake batter at the windows. "Give them back!"

The two raccoons spotted the movement and suddenly realized there were people in the house. They whooshed back along the deck and disappeared.

"What did raccoons want your sneakers for?" Lucy glanced back at Reuben, bewildered. She was pretty sure sneakers were the same thing as trainers, but she wondered if she'd mixed the words up.

"No idea. But they definitely took them," Reuben shrugged.

"Everyone knows raccoons like stuff that stinks," Sam pointed out, walking into the kitchen with Jack trailing after him and grabbing a plate for pancakes.

"They were almost new!" Reuben protested.

"So you shouldn't have left them on the deck for raccoons to steal." Auntie Cass sighed. "Seriously, Jack and Lucy, don't leave stuff outside – always bring it in."

Shadow had been watching the raccoons with his ears laid back and his tail fluffed up. Now that they'd gone, he padded over to the glass doors and stood up, stretching full length and patting at the handle.

"Shall I let him out?" Lucy asked, but Auntie Cass and her cousins were all still talking about Reuben's sneakers and how unfair it was that he'd had to pay for new ones (Reuben) and how of course he had to pay for them when he'd been silly enough to leave them outside (everyone else).

Shadow was looking desperate to get out so Lucy decided she'd better just open the door.

He stared up at her curiously as she twisted the handle and when she slid it open he didn't rush out straight away, as Billy would have done. He almost looked surprised. Lucy eyed him worriedly, and then looked back at the others. "Auntie Cass…"

"Oh! Don't let him out, Lucy."

"Too late." Sam darted across the room and rugby-tackled Shadow just as he got to the edge of the deck. There was a thump and a faint, grumpy mew before Sam marched back in, dangling Shadow under his front paws.

"Sorry, we should have told you," Auntie Cass said, hurrying over to shut the door again behind him. She turned round and smiled at Lucy but she still looked a bit worried. "Is he OK, Sam?"

"He's fine – what about *me*?" Sam rolled
his eyes. "The deck's hard!" He put Shadow
down and the grey cat stalked away crossly.

Lucy thought he was probably just as embarrassed as she was.

"He's not allowed out?" she faltered.

"No – and don't worry, I know you were only trying to help. He does try to sneak out whenever he gets a chance," Auntie Cass explained. "It might sound like everything round here is dangerous, but it is, in a way… Because we live really close to the forest – almost in it, I guess – we have to keep Shadow as an indoor cat. There's a lot of wildlife out there that could hurt him."

"Like bears?" Lucy asked, glancing worriedly at the glass doors.

"I'm not sure a bear would bother," Auntie Cass said. "But we have coyotes – they're like wild dogs – and there are eagles as well. They're definitely a risk to pets."

Lucy's eyes widened as she imagined an eagle swooping down to grab Shadow.

"And cougars," Reuben added. "Big cats."

Jack and Lucy exchanged a glance. Auntie Cass was right, Lucy thought. At this rate, she wasn't sure she wanted to step outdoors...

Mum and Dad woke up a little later, and though they'd missed the pancakes, Jack made Auntie Cass promise to make them again – so Mum and Dad didn't miss out, obviously.

Uncle Pete suggested a walk up one of the forest trails that afternoon. Lucy was still a bit worried about bears and cougars and coyotes and eagles – but no one else seemed to be, not even Jack. Their Canadian cousins were outdoorsy and used to hiking. At home Lucy's family did go for walks, but mostly when they were on holiday and visiting somewhere special. Then again, if they had a forest and mountains practically in their back garden, she was sure they'd do more walking too. They didn't even have to drive to get to this trail – it was close enough to walk from the house. They set off up a little tarmac road, heading past a few other houses set deep in the trees.

"I can't believe this is just on your doorstep," Dad said, as the tarmac petered out and they came on to a rocky trail. It was starting to feel much wilder now, the trees tall and dark. Lucy couldn't hear any cars at all.

"We're not going too far," Uncle Pete told them. "You can take this trail all the way up the side of the mountain, but that's a long hike. Not for your first day!"

Lucy shook her head, relieved. Perhaps they could work up to it, though. She liked the idea of climbing a mountain and looking down on the forest, all the way to the sea. The trail was already steep though and she was starting to feel a bit out of breath. She stopped to pull her water bottle out of the side of her backpack and Kitty stopped too, calling to Uncle Pete.

"Dad! Hang on!"

Uncle Pete turned back, smiling. "Sorry! Was I going too fast? I always forget I've got longer legs."

"You don't have to wait for me," Lucy said, feeling embarrassed. She hadn't meant to hold everyone back. "I can catch up in a minute."

Kitty shook her head. "Uh-uh. We can't leave you behind. Not out here. We have to stay together."

"She's right." Uncle Pete grinned and gave
Sam and Reuben a pointed sort of look. "In fact,
I reckon we're far enough along the trail that we
should probably start singing."

Both boys groaned and Lucy's mum raised her eyebrows. "Singing? I'm out of breath already..."

"That's me racing off too fast. We'll have a breather and then set off again more slowly," Uncle Pete said encouragingly. "I'm serious about the singing, though. We've never actually spotted a bear along here, but they are about."

Lucy looked round, her heart suddenly beating faster. All the tree shadows seemed thicker and darker now. As if they might be hiding a bear lurking there, watching them...

"I don't get the singing," Lucy's dad said, shaking his head. "I mean, I know your voice is awful, but is it really going to send a bear running...?"

Uncle Pete rolled his eyes at him. "It doesn't have to be singing, it's just easy." He nudged Sam.

"And it means I get to embarrass the kids. Any loud noise will do – we want the bears to know we're coming." He smiled. "Don't worry. They don't want to chase us or anything like that. Bears are all about the eating and they'd much rather eat fish or berries than us. Mostly they want to be left alone. If they can hear us coming, they'll stay out of our way, you see?"

"So we have to listen to Dad singing…" Sam sighed.

"Worse, you have to join in." Uncle Pete rubbed his hands together. "I'm going to start with my Disney selection, I think. How about 'Let it Go'?"

Everyone groaned and Reuben and Sam started chanting some weird song they said they'd learned in Scouts instead.

Uncle Pete dropped back to walk next to Lucy and her mum. "You're not worried about the bears, are you?" he asked. "I didn't mean to scare you. There's a whole lot of precautions we take, but it's just to be safe."

"I'm sort of scared," Lucy admitted. "But … I do wish we could see a bear as well. If it was safe."

"We can go to Grouse Mountain," Auntie Cass called back. "It's on our list of trips to take you guys on! There's a cable car to get up to the top, with amazing views back to the city. But best of all they have a bear sanctuary, with two grizzlies."

"Yeah, they're really cute," Kitty agreed. "They have a pond and one of them just spends the whole day lying in it."

"That sounds good," Lucy said slowly. And it

did – but even in that frightened moment, when all those shadows behind the trees had claws, she had felt a little whisper of excitement. A bear. A real bear. A *wild* bear.

Then again, that probably meant she was being one of the careless trippers who "got into trouble", as Uncle Pete put it.

"Dad!" Reuben had been walking at the front with Lucy's dad, but now he stopped, pointing at one of the trees. "Look! Do you reckon that looks fresh?"

Uncle Pete strode over and everyone else followed, staring at the deep scratches cut into the fir tree. The bark was hanging off in long ribbons, showing the pale wood beneath. Even Lucy – who didn't know much about bears or trees – could see that something very tall had scraped its claws down the tree, probably not very long ago. The wood was so fresh it looked damp.

But – the claw marks were so high up. Higher than Dad and Uncle Pete's heads. How big was the bear that had made them?

"There's fur on there too," Lucy said and her voice came out a bit wobbly. She pointed further round the tree, a little lower down, where great clumps of dark fur had matted into the bark.

"Mmm…" Uncle Pete said, looking up and down the trail. "Bears like to scratch their itchy backs sometimes. Sorry, everyone. I had planned on taking a circular route, but I think we're better off heading back down the way we came."

"Because there's a bear?" Jack asked, wide-eyed.

Uncle Pete nodded. "I checked the website and there weren't any trail closures because of bear activity but Reuben's right, that does look fresh, so one could be around. Bears are more likely to be out at dawn and dusk, so there's a few hours to go, but still... We're better off going back the same way we came. The bear could be somewhere up ahead of us."

"That sounds like a very good idea," Mum said – and her voice was just as wobbly as Lucy's had been.

"Don't worry." Auntie Cass put a hand on Mum's arm. "We're probably being too cautious – but better safe than sorry. And the good thing is, we'll have time to take a quick trip down to the beach instead," she added, smiling at Jack and Lucy.

"Good plan." Uncle Pete set off back down

the trail. "I'm going on to musicals now, you lot. What shall we start with? *Hamilton*? *Wicked*? Or we could skip straight to Reuben's favourite and go for *The Sound of Music…*"

The beach was beautiful – soft, grey-gold sand scattered with huge driftwood logs. Lucy and Mum spread out beach mats by one of the logs and leaned against it, watching the dark blue water.

"I've worked out what's so strange," Mum said at last. "The islands. Whenever we've been to the seaside back home, you can see the sea stretching out in front of you. But here you're looking at sea and then mountains."

"Yes!" Lucy sat up. She'd been thinking the same. "It makes the beach feel almost like a jungle, with all the trees and the mountains in front."

"Come and swim, Lucy," Kitty called, running down the beach towards the water. "There's a special pool, it's really safe."

Lucy wriggled out of the T-shirt and shorts she'd put on over her swimming costume and followed Kitty down the beach. More long tree trunks had been fastened together in the water to make a barrier around a huge square of sea. There was even a floating platform to swim out to. Lucy loved swimming, and swimming in the sea was even better than a pool. The only problem was she hated going out of her depth and she kept on having to stop and put her feet down just in case. Every so often she'd try to touch the bottom, and then have that horrible feeling when it wasn't there and the water went up over her nose. But here it looked like you couldn't swim out too far. She could relax and mess around with Kitty and the others.

"Wow, you're fast!" Kitty said admiringly as Lucy raced after Jack when he'd splashed her.

"I love swimming." Lucy turned on to her back to float and stare up at the sky. "I think I'd be on the beach every day if we lived here."

Kitty giggled. "Maybe in the summer. Actually, there are some people who swim in the winter too but they mostly have wetsuits. It doesn't get as cold here as it does in some parts of Canada, but it rains a *lot*."

"Kitty!" Auntie Cass was standing at the edge of the water and waving at them. "I had a message from Martha's mom. Do you want to go over to theirs tomorrow? She's invited Lucy too."

"Yes!" Kitty bounced in the water, sending a wave splashing over Lucy. "Oops, sorry. But that's OK with you, isn't it? Martha's great, you'll love her. And she's got a pool in her back yard too."

Lucy nodded. A pool sounded good – but she wasn't sure about spending time with one of Kitty's friends when she didn't even know Kitty that well yet. She couldn't really say that though, could she?

Martha turned out to be just as nice as Kitty had promised. She loved Lucy's English accent and kept making her say things and telling her how cute it was. She was a bit disappointed that Lucy had never met anyone from the royal family, though. She seemed to think that everyone who lived in Britain was at Buckingham Palace having tea with the King every week. Lucy told her about visiting the Tower of London with school but it wasn't quite as impressive.

"I think it's more exciting that you've got bears and cougars and wolves and things," she told Martha as they lounged around the edge of the pool, paddling their feet in the cool water. "I'd rather see a bear than royalty."

Martha looked shocked, as though she didn't think that was the proper attitude at all. "No!" Then she suddenly laughed and held up one hand. "Hang on." She dashed inside the house and came back dragging her mum, who smiled at Lucy.

"Martha says I've got to show you this," she explained, pulling her phone out of her pocket. "It's from a few years ago now but Martha's dad put it on YouTube." She frowned at the screen and then nodded. "Here you go." She held the phone out so the girls could see it and turned the volume up.

Lucy leaned in, looking at the slightly wobbly video. It was a garden – this garden, she realized after a couple of seconds. The same pool they were sitting around now. "That's here?"

"Uh-huh – keep watching – I think I was so excited it took me a moment to focus in properly."

Lucy squeaked suddenly, and Martha and her mum laughed. "Yeah, that's what I was like," Martha's mum agreed.

"There's a bear in your garden!"

"It gets even better," Martha told her smugly. "You watch."

The bear was so gorgeous, Lucy thought. Plump and shiny black and cuddly looking. It actually looked quite like the huge toy bear she had on her bed back home. It lumbered round the side of the pool, then dipped one huge front paw and started splashing.

"It was so hot that summer," Martha's mother explained. "I think he was trying to cool down."

"Ahhh, he's getting in!" Lucy gasped,

watching as the
bear slipped
into the pool
and lounged
against the side,
enjoying the cool
water. Then he
turned round and
put both paws on
the edge and rested
his nose on them.

"He's just chilling," Kitty said, giggling. "Oh,
look at him shake!"

The bear had clambered out of the pool now
and was shaking himself dry like a huge dog.
Then he turned, looking towards the camera.

"This is where he spotted us," Martha's mum
said. "He was a bit shy. And there he goes.

Right through the fence." She sighed and shook her head. "Still, it was amazing to see. We did worry that he might keep coming back and break the fence down again, but he never did. We didn't let Martha play in the back yard for a while, though."

"That was amazing," Lucy told her.

"It was," Martha's mum agreed. "Terrifying but amazing too. OK, I'm going to go and make some sandwiches for you girls. Watch out for those bears now…"

Lucy looked around the yard, imagining a bear crashing through the fence.

"It's OK," Martha said. "Like Mom said, he never came back. But we do get bears wandering down the street every so often."

Lucy thought she sounded very calm about it. "Just … just walking down the street?"

"Uh-huh."

"I can't believe you're all so *Oh, I just saw a bear in my swimming pool, how's your day going?*" Lucy said. "I think I'd probably run away if I saw a grizzly bear."

Martha shook her head and Kitty said, "No, what we get around here are mostly *black* bears. I don't think I've *ever* seen a grizzly – not a wild one. When we saw those claw marks yesterday, Dad thought they might be from a grizzly because they were really high up and grizzlies are bigger than black bears."

"They can get really big," Martha agreed.

"And a grizzly bear might attack if she's got cubs. Not because they're mean, it's only if people get in their space. Or they're scared for their babies."

Lucy frowned. "So black bears don't do

that?" She was getting confused. She hadn't realized there were two different sorts of bears around here, and now it was getting even more complicated. "How do you know all this stuff?"

"We get wildlife ambassadors coming into school," Martha explained. "And whenever there's a carnival or something, they always have a stall with leaflets and bear spray you can pick up."

"Black bears send their cubs up trees," Kitty put in. "That's what they do when they're off looking for food – the mom finds a big pine tree and the cubs mostly stay up the tree and sleep. And if the cubs are playing on the ground they can get up the tree and stay safe. Grizzlies can climb too but they're not as fast as black bears and they don't tree their cubs. So sometimes a hiker might get in between a grizzly mom and her babies, and that's not good."

"But you shouldn't ever climb a tree to get away from a bear," Martha added, giggling. "Because the bear's going to be better at climbing than you are and then there's you and a bear, stuck up a tree!"

"What are you supposed to do then?" Lucy said, almost in a wail. She felt like she needed a bear handbook.

Kitty and Martha looked at each other and grinned, and then Kitty held up one hand and started ticking things off on her fingers. "Don't run," she said seriously. "Or scream. Bears are really fast and you don't want them to think you're food they should chase. You have to try and make yourself look scarier than a bear – that's why it's always good to go hiking in a group and not on your own. Stand tall and talk calmly to the bear so it knows you're a human and not something it wants to eat and start backing away."

Martha nodded. "If you meet a grizzly with cubs and she attacks you, lie down on the ground, put your hands over your head and play dead. Not if it's a black bear, though – for them you have to try and get away to somewhere safe and if you can't, then you fight back."

"Fight … a *bear*?" Lucy stared at the other two in disbelief. They weren't serious, were they?

"Yeah…" Kitty shrugged. "I know it sounds weird. You're supposed to try and smack them in the face with whatever you've got – like, I don't know – a water bottle?"

Martha snorted with laughter and that set them all off, just imagining trying to fight an angry bear with whatever they might be carrying.

"Or a hat!" Lucy wheezed.

"Your phone!"

"I suppose at least it's easy to tell the difference between them," Lucy said at last, still breathless from laughing. "To know whether you should fight or not, I mean."

"Uh-uh." Martha shook her head.

"But – black bears are black. It's in the name! And grizzly bears are brown, aren't they?"

"Mostly they're brown, but they can be really pale, almost blond. And black bears can be brown too."

"Why are they called black bears then?" Lucy said, rolling her eyes.

"You need to check if the bear's got a hump on its shoulders," Martha explained. "Then it's a grizzly. And black bears have much bigger ears, and a different shape to their nose – like long and smooth and sloping, instead of having a teddy bear snout like a grizzly does."

Lucy shook her head. "Maybe I won't be going on any more hikes with you lot."

"Good luck with that," Kitty said. "Dad's got plans. We're going camping too."

"Camping in a forest full of bears!" Lucy squeaked. After all Kitty and Martha's talk about playing dead and being chased up trees, it really didn't sound like a good idea.

"It's OK, honestly," Martha told her. "We're more dangerous to the bears than they are to us."

"Not me," Lucy said sadly, shaking her head. "I definitely can't hit a bear in the face, Martha, even if you could."

"Ummm, me neither. Although I guess you never know what you can do until you have to." Martha sighed. "No, I meant that we're living where the bears want to be. My mom was telling me about it ages ago when I said I wished that bear would come and swim in the pool again. I was too young to really remember it much and the video's so sweet. Mom told me it was cute and funny but it wasn't really good because it meant the bear might get used to coming close to people and then he'd do it more and more until he comes too close and someone scares him maybe, so he gets fierce." She sighed. "And that's when he's in trouble because no one's going to let a bear just attack people and get away with it, are they?"

Lucy looked at her blankly. She wasn't really sure what Martha meant.

"Conservation officers have to shoot problem bears," Kitty told her. "That's one of the things the wildlife ambassadors always explain when they come and do talks for us in school. If we leave rubbish around or don't clean up a barbecue grill or – or have lots of bird feeders even – that brings the bears to us. And that's fine once in a while when they're being cute and people can take photos. But the bears start to like human food and the other stuff we've left lying around, and then they keep coming back."

"Why do they have to shoot them?" Lucy asked sadly. "Why don't they just move them on somewhere else? Don't they have those dart guns to send the bear to sleep so they can move them?"

"But they'd just come back," Kitty said. "Or a different bear would. It's better to get rid of the garbage or the pet food or whatever."

"Girls!" Martha's mum came dashing out into the garden. "Come and see! There's a bear down the street, one of the neighbours just called me. I think we'll be able to see it if we stand on the balcony." She hurried them through the house and unlocked the door to the little balcony. "We have breakfast out here sometimes," she explained to Lucy. "Oh, look there, can you see?" She pointed to a small tree that was growing on a lawn a few houses down, just next to the road. The tree was shaking wildly – because there was a large bear halfway up it.

THE LOST BEAR CUB

"That's really a bear," Lucy whispered. She couldn't stop staring. It was only about fifty metres away, just messing around in a tree. There were people standing on the pavement filming it with their phones and a guy on a bike had stopped in the middle of the road to watch.

"I told you they came wandering down the street," Martha said smugly.

"Is it eating the leaves?" Lucy asked. She knew koalas and pandas ate leaves but she hadn't thought all bears did.

Martha's mum sighed. "No, I think it's eating cherries – I'm pretty sure that's a cherry tree. It shouldn't be planted here, we're not supposed to have fruit trees."

"Because of bears?"

"Exactly. That's just a bear snack waiting to happen."

Lucy stifled a laugh – the bear was funny, chomping away at the cherries on the leafy branches. The tree was so small, only about twice as tall as the bear – every time he reached out a paw to pull a branch closer the whole thing swayed. But everything Kitty and Martha had said about bears getting to like human food and then coming back for more was worrying her. What if the bear took a swipe at one of those people watching and someone called the police or the conservation officers that Kitty had talked about?

"That's a black bear, right?" she whispered to her cousin. The girls had said they never saw grizzlies around and she *thought* the bear had a sloping nose. It definitely had that same beautiful shining black fur, like the bear in the pool video.

"Yes. Oh!" Kitty yelped as the tree suddenly shook even more and there was a loud splintering noise. The bear had leaned over just too far, and it was too much for the branch it was perched on. It peeled away from the trunk and the bear did a sort of slow-motion controlled fall, sliding down the trunk and gathering more branches on the way. It ended up sitting on its bottom on the grass in a pile of leaves and twigs. Lucy thought it looked surprised and maybe a little bit embarrassed.

One of the guys with phones suddenly realized he was very close and backed off – but the bear didn't seem bothered. It lumbered up and clearly decided to make the best of a bad job. It stuck its nose in among the branches it had accidentally pulled down, snuffling around for more cherries. It seemed determined not to miss any.

What Lucy couldn't get over was that the bear was right next to the pavement – the sidewalk, she guessed she should probably call it. Someone could just be walking home from school, chatting to friends, and suddenly they'd find a bear right there!

"I don't think the tree's ever coming back from that," Martha said, shaking her head. It looked more like a pile of broken branches now than a tree.

The bear seemed to think so too. It walked carefully round the mess, checking to see if it had missed any delicious fruit, then sauntered off down the street.

"Where's it going?" Lucy asked.

"There's a stream that runs down the end there," Martha's mother said. "It could easily follow it back towards the mountain." She smiled at Lucy. "You can tell the rest of your family you saw something pretty special." She held her phone out to show Lucy a photo – the three girls watching wide-eyed, with the bear sitting on the grass in the background, looking a bit confused. "I'll send it to your mom, Kitty, and she can share it with Lucy's mom and dad."

"Thank you! I love it!" Lucy smiled at her. "I hope the bear's going to be OK," she added, looking worriedly down the road again.

"Me too." Martha's mum nodded. "Try not to worry, Lucy. I reckon it just saw a quick snack and took it. The Carmichaels, they're the family that live in that house, they're definitely going to get rid of the tree. The bear won't be tempted to do that again."

Lucy nodded. She really hoped so.

Uncle Pete had planned the camping trip
for the weekend. It was going to be just
him, Auntie Cass and all the cousins so
Lucy's mum and dad could spend some time
together exploring Vancouver.

Lucy was doing her best to think about
all the fun things they were going to do –
cooking marshmallows over a fire, going on
a canoe trip on the lake – instead of worrying
about wild creatures in the forest on the other
side of a flimsy bit of fabric. Auntie Cass had
explained that knowing they were so close to

wildlife was part of what made camping so special. Lucy *was* excited. But then she kept remembering how big that bear by Martha's house had been, the way the little tree had collapsed underneath it.

She went to talk to Jack about it all when they were packing to leave. Sam had disappeared to find his washed clothes so Jack was on his own in Sam's room.

"Hey…"

Her brother looked up. "You OK? Can you remember what Uncle Pete said we should take to wear for canoeing?"

"Um, just a T-shirt and shorts, I think. Jack … are you worried about sleeping in a tent?"

"No. We did it with Scouts. It's fun, you'll love it. And Uncle Pete said their tent's really nice. Me, Sam and Reuben have to sleep in the old one, and Sam told me it leaks!"

"There were no bears where you went with Scouts though."

"I still can't believe you saw a bear at Kitty's friend's house." Jack sighed. "It's so unfair." Then he frowned at her. "Are you really scared about it?"

"Don't tell the others!" Lucy said pleadingly. She and Jack usually got on well, but he did tease her sometimes. She could just imagine him telling Reuben and Sam that Lucy was being a baby – trying to impress their big cousins. "I've never slept in a tent. Isn't it weird, not being in a house? A tent's just fabric. It's like sleeping under a big umbrella."

"I won't tell anyone. It's OK, Lucy. Uncle Pete and Auntie Cass know what they're doing, they've been camping loads of times."

"Uncle Pete had a bear break into his car!"
Lucy pointed out.

"I know, but that was his old car and it was
years ago, when he first moved here. It's going
to be fine. We'll just see deer and stuff. Maybe
eagles. Uncle Pete said you can see them
flying over the campsite. That'll be cool."

Lucy nodded, feeling a little better. Jack was
right. Everything was going to be fine.

The campsite they were going to wasn't far
away but they were taking two cars to fit all
seven people and two tents, plus a whole lot
of other camping stuff – mats and sleeping
bags and camping chairs and cool boxes with
food in.

"It's really beautiful at Gardner Lake,"
Auntie Cass told Lucy as they drove there.
"Isn't it, Kitty?"

"Yeah, it's great. You can camp really
close to the water and there's a place to hire
paddleboards and canoes, but you don't even
need to do that. It's fun just kind of messing
about by the lake."

"I love going to sleep listening to the water
and the birds," Auntie Cass said. "It's so
peaceful, even with these three around."

"Hey…" But Kitty sounded as though she
didn't really mind. "Look – that's a sign for
the campground, we're nearly there!"

Lucy saw a narrow road turning off in
among the trees and excitement started to
bubble up inside her. The afternoon sun was
gleaming through the leaves so they were

driving through dappled shadows and it made everything look mysterious. The only sign that people had been there was the road itself – everything else was just tall trees and ferns and a few huge rocks dotted around.

And then the trees opened out to a clearing along the side of a wide, still lake, glittering in the sunlight.

"Oh, wow…" Lucy whispered. She could see why Kitty and Auntie Cass had been so excited – there was something magical about the lake stretching out in front of them with the tall trees behind it.

Lucy and Kitty climbed out of the car and ran to stand at the water's edge. It was so still that Lucy could see the trees and the mountains reflected on the surface.

Now that she looked around, she could see

there were small buildings here and there –
a toilet block, she guessed, and some storage
lockers. She could see a few other brightly
coloured tents further along the shore

THE LOST BEAR CUB

of the lake and there was a dock with a sign
advertising canoes and paddleboards. But it
didn't take away from the peaceful wildness
of it all.

Uncle Pete's car drew up beside theirs, and Sam, Reuben and Jack spilled out, whooping excitedly. Jack grabbed Lucy and swung her around. She laughed, catching his wild mood.

They pitched the two tents not far from the edge of the water and laid out sleeping bags ready for the evening. Uncle Pete got out a Frisbee, and everyone played for a while, even though the Frisbee seemed to end up in the lake every second throw, and someone had to go splashing in after it.

Lucy collapsed on one of the camping chairs after a while, worn out by racing in and out of the water. She offered to help Auntie Cass set up the gas camping stove and make pasta for dinner, but there wasn't much that needed doing, so she wandered along the waterline instead, picking up interesting pebbles and

trying to spot fish
further out in the
lake. She was sure
she could hear
them, little splashes
and plops every so
often, and she could
see rings of ripples
where they'd dived
back under the surface.

She could hear the
others, still laughing and
shouting excitedly as they
chased after the Frisbee – teasing Jack after
he'd nearly fallen and soaked his clothes. Lucy
smiled and walked on, leaning down to pick up
a bit of driftwood that had been softened and
smoothed by the lapping water.

Then she stood up again, slowly, caught by the strange feeling that someone was watching her. There was only a narrow stretch of sand and stone here, between the water and the trees, narrow enough that the shade of the tree branches made her feel suddenly cold. She saw the hairs on her arms rise and she shivered.

Standing by the trunk of the nearest tree, only a few metres away, was a small black bear.

Lucy froze and so did the bear. They stared at each other and Lucy tried desperately to remember what everyone had said about bears and what to do if you meet one. *Large ears. Very black fur.* She couldn't see a hump above its shoulders, but then that was probably because it was facing her. Lucy's mind squeaked and skittered. If it was a black bear did that mean she was supposed to play dead, or run?

What do I do?

Stand tall and try to be scary. Show the bear you're human.

"Go away, bear!" she said in a small voice. Then she coughed and tried to say it louder. "I'm not something to eat. Go away, bear!"

The bear just stared at her as though it had no idea *what* she was.

It was very small, Lucy realized. Definitely a lot smaller than the one they'd seen in the cherry tree. In fact, now she was a tiny bit calmer, Lucy could see that the bear was a cub. If it stood on its hind paws, it would probably still be shorter than she was. And it was very sweet – like a teddy bear, with those big, round ears standing up and the paler brown muzzle. It had a little white spot on the front of its chest, almost like it was wearing a pendant.

Lucy's heart slowed a little and she managed to take a deep, proper breath. Just because the bear was little, that didn't mean she was safe. It still had claws – she could see them, hooked and sharp. But it wasn't that which was worrying her. The cub must have a mother and she was probably close by. Probably she was looking for her cub right now! Lucy gulped. *Don't get between a cub and its mother*, Kitty and Martha had said. Shouldn't this cub be safe up a tree somewhere? Lucy looked wildly around and then up, as if the mother bear was about to come clambering down from the tree above.

The cub looked up too, uncertainly, and something twisted inside Lucy – all of a sudden, she was scared for the bear, as well as for herself. His little furred face looked so worried.

"I'm not going to hurt you," she told him, almost without meaning to. "Where's your mother gone? Are you looking for her? Are you lost?"

"Lucy!" someone called, their voice low and anxious.

Lucy glanced sideways and saw Uncle Pete, with Jack and her cousins gathered close behind him. Jack looked utterly panicked – Reuben was actually holding on to him to stop him rushing towards her.

"I think the cub might be lost," she said, looking back – just as the bear turned tail and disappeared into the bushes.

Jack broke free and hurled himself at Lucy, grabbing her tightly. "Are you OK? It didn't hurt you?"

"I'm fine… He was only little."

Uncle Pete shook his head. "But its mom is probably close by. Come on, all of you," he said, sounding grim. "We're heading back to the tents. I'd better warn the other campers that

there are bears around. Come on, Lucy," he
added, quite sharply, as she lingered to watch
the bushes where the bear cub had disappeared.
"You shouldn't have been all the way over
here on your own! You know we said everyone
needed to stay together."

"Sorry…" Lucy ducked her head. She *had*
known that – but it wasn't as if she'd gone very
far. She'd only been looking for pebbles.

Uncle Pete sighed. "I'm not cross with you.
It's just – we were really worried. You can't
wander off, it's not safe. What if I had to go
back to your mom and tell her you'd been eaten
by a bear!" he added. He was trying to sound
jokey and funny, but he was really upset, Lucy
realized.

"Sorry," she said again, meaning it this time.
"I'll be more careful. I didn't see the mother

bear, Uncle Pete. Just the little one. He didn't want to hurt me, I'm sure of it."

"Probably not," Uncle Pete agreed. "But you can't predict what a wild creature's going to do, Lucy. Just please stay close from now on."

The mood at the campsite had changed since Lucy's bear encounter. Uncle Pete was still silent and worried – he and Auntie Cass went over by the cars and had a long discussion. Even without being able to hear what they were saying, Lucy could tell it was serious.

"They're trying to decide whether we should go home," Kitty said, and she looked at Lucy as she said it. Lucy swallowed guiltily. Maybe they ought to go home, if there were bears around the campsite?

"Because it's not safe?" she asked uncertainly.

"No! Because you went wandering off and they can't trust you!" Kitty snapped.

"Hey…" Jack said. "Don't be mean to her."

"I'm not!" Kitty rolled her eyes. "I'm just saying what happened."

"She didn't mean to, Kitty," Reuben said, with enough big-brotherly authority to send Kitty stomping into the tent. Lucy heard the flump of her sleeping bag as she flung herself down on it in a huff and a loud whisper-that-was-meant-to-be-heard of, "Ruined everything!"

That sleeping bag was next to the one she was supposed to sleep in tonight. Lucy looked round at Auntie Cass and Uncle Pete again, really hoping they would decide everyone had to go home. She didn't want to spend the night squished up in a tent next to a furious cousin.

But if they went home Kitty would be even

crosser. Lucy sighed. "I'm sorry," she said
to Reuben and Sam. "I didn't mean to spoil
things."

Reuben was looking at his parents. "It's
OK. I reckon we're staying. Dad hasn't got
that bad-news look on his face." He grinned
at Lucy. "But no more chasing after *lost* bear
cubs, OK?"

Sam snorted. "Yeah, it's OK, Lucy. We'll
make him a map." He grabbed a stick and
started drawing in the damp sand at the edge
of the water, a huge arrow, and then HOME
in big letters. Lucy tried to laugh – Reuben
and Jack were laughing – but she didn't think
it was very funny.

"Dinner!" Auntie Cass said cheerfully as she
and Uncle Pete came back to the tents. "It's all
ready. Where's Kitty?"

"I'm here!" Kitty came out of the tent looking hopeful. "So we're not going home?"

Auntie Cass sighed and exchanged a glance with Uncle Pete. Perhaps they'd thought no one knew what they were talking about. "No. Everything's fine. We're having dinner and then maybe we can do some stargazing as it's going to be a really clear night. But we must be extra careful with the clearing up since we know there are bears around. We need to bag up all our rubbish." She smiled at Lucy and Jack. "We even have to strain any bits of food out of the washing-up water and make sure we bag them up too. But it'll be worth it. Just wait till later on when you're eating a s'more and looking at the stars."

She passed out bowls of pasta and tomato sauce and Lucy settled into her camp chair to eat, glancing at Kitty every so often. Was her cousin still cross with her? It was hard to tell.

"I guess the stars are different here," Kitty said and Lucy felt the worried knot inside her ease away. Maybe they weren't going to talk about the argument, but she didn't mind, not that much. She just wanted Kitty not to be angry. She dug her fork into her pasta, suddenly hungry again.

Jack turned out to be right about sleeping in a tent. It wasn't scary. Somehow even just that thin wall of fabric was enough to make Lucy feel safe. She lay there listening to the soft lap of the lake water against the shore and wondering how long it would take her to get to sleep – and then she woke up and it was light again, and Kitty had rolled over in the night and squashed her up against the side of the tent.

Lucy wriggled out from half underneath her cousin and unzipped the door of their little bedroom and then the main door. The lake was a quiet grey under a wispy layer of early morning mist and Auntie Cass was standing by the edge, gazing at the water. Lucy stood there watching – she didn't want to break the moment. There was something magical about the gentle call of the water.

Auntie Cass looked round and jumped as she saw Lucy. "You're up early!" she said, laughing. "I'm just going to the locker to get the breakfast things. Do you want to come and help? You'll need your shoes."

Lucy nodded and ducked back into the tent to grab her trainers. Then she followed Auntie Cass along a path that led to the toilets and showers – and a set of big metal cases.

"Are those the lockers? I wasn't sure what they were for."

"Yup. They're bear-proof, there's one for each pitch on the campsite." Auntie Cass unlatched the doors and reached in to push the lid off the cool box. "Here you go – can you put all this in the bag for me?" She handed out milk and juice and cereal, and lots of other bits. "It's much safer having something like this to store your food in. You can keep things in the trunk of the car as long as it's all really well sealed. But after Pete told me that story about the bear getting into his car, I just don't like to risk it."

They went on a long walk around the lake shore after breakfast and then came back to take the tents down and pack everything away in the car before they went canoeing. Lucy had done canoeing with school – part of their activities week back at the end of the summer term, so not that long before. It was good to actually know what she was doing – it meant she didn't feel that Kitty and the others had to tell her *everything*.

Reuben, Sam and Jack shared one big, open

canoe, and Lucy and Kitty went with Auntie Cass and Uncle Pete in two smaller ones. Lucy was glad when Kitty begged to go with Uncle Pete – she was still a bit worried that he was annoyed with her about wandering off.

"It feels different to when we did it with school," Lucy told Auntie Cass as they paddled away from the busy dock. "That was on a lake too but it was tiny! And there were lots of

reeds and water plants so you couldn't really see down into the water. This is so clear, I can see the stones at the bottom." Then she squeaked excitedly. "I saw a fish!"

Auntie Cass laughed. "There's a lot of them down there…"

"But it was huge!" Lucy twisted round, trying to see where the fish had gone, and the canoe wobbled a bit. "Sorry!"

"It's OK – we've never managed to capsize these big canoes so far. They're really flat on the base so it stops them tipping. Sometimes I think Sam and Reuben are trying to, though."

Lucy nodded and dug her paddle in to catch up with the others. They were paddling past tall grey rocks now, with the odd pine tree perched here and there. It seemed to be a part of the lake that would be hard to reach by land – Lucy felt like an explorer. "Is that a waterfall?" she called back to Auntie Cass as they came round the rocks and she saw white water spilling down into the lake.

"Yes, that's one of the rivers that fills the lake," Auntie Cass yelled over the noise of the water. "We're going to stop for a picnic on the other side."

They beached the canoes on a tiny patch
of muddy shingle, not that far beyond the
waterfall, and then climbed over the rocks to
sit just above the pouring water and eat their
lunch. Auntie Cass had brought it with them
in a bear-proof canister – Lucy had thought
it was a water barrel when she first saw it in
the car.

"This is the best place I've eaten lunch, ever,"
Jack said, taking another bite of his roll.

Uncle Pete laughed. "I don't know, it's a bit
noisy. But yeah, it's amazing…" He trailed
off, glancing around, and then said, "Hey…
Listen…"

Lucy couldn't hear much above the water
at first, but then she caught a chirping cry –
a little bit like a seagull. "What is it?"

"There – up in that tree, can you see?"

Uncle Pete pointed to a tall tree just on the other side of the waterfall, and Lucy gulped. There was an enormous, dark-feathered bird perched on one of the branches.

"An eagle!"

Uncle Pete nodded. "Keep watching. It might go fishing – they live mostly on fish, and it's amazing if you can see them at it."

"There's another one!" Jack said suddenly, pointing out across the water. "There, in the sky! It *is* another eagle, isn't it? Wow, look at the wings! It's huge!"

"And the claws!" Lucy gasped, as the gliding eagle seemed to change shape entirely in the air – the black-feathered legs swung down, tipped with huge yellow talons, and it snatched something silvery from the water. "It's got a fish!"

The eagle kept flying towards them, clearly making for the same tree. Perhaps the other eagle was its mate? As it flew, it tipped its legs forwards again and took the fish in its beak, gulping it down.

"Never seen that before," Uncle Pete said, laughing. "Pretty impressive to manage that and fly at the same time!"

The two eagles sat in the tree for a while longer and then glided over the lake together. Lucy frowned. "They're not bald at all! Their heads have got white feathers on them."

"I guess they just look bald," Sam agreed.

Kitty shook her head. "We learned about it at school. It's short for piebald – that means kind of patchy."

"We should head back." Auntie Cass stood up and stretched, and then started to pack all the leftover food and wrappers back into the bear-proof canister.

They cut back straight across the lake this time, instead of following the shore – it was amazing to be out on the glittering water with birds swooping overhead. They saw the eagles in the distance, riding on the thermals above the lake. Lucy hoped they'd come closer – she wanted to see them fishing again – but they seemed to be enjoying cruising instead.

The day out on the water had left Lucy weary, but in a good way. She had a feeling her arms might hurt the next morning, and her legs were shaky from sitting hunched up on the little seat in the canoe. They wobbled when she stood up by the dock to get out.

"The eagles are back!" Reuben called, pointing excitedly, and Lucy swung round to look.

THE LOST BEAR CUB

She just caught a glimpse of the birds skimming over the water before the canoe swung underneath her, and she tipped slowly and splashily into the lake.

"Lucy!" Auntie Cass yelped, nearly falling in herself as she tried to grab her.

Lucy bobbed in the water, her buoyancy aid helping her to float. It had ridden up and settled weirdly under her chin. She gripped the side of the canoe and wondered how she was supposed to get back in.

"Are you OK?" Jack yelled, and Lucy nodded and spluttered at him. Some lake had gone up her nose.

"Swim along the side of the canoe to the deck." Auntie Cass pointed. "There's a ladder, and it'll be easier for us to help you get out."

Lucy floundered along past the canoe and tried to pull her wobbly legs up the ladder. It didn't work very well but Sam and Reuben and Uncle Pete hauled her out. She stood dripping on the dock and Sam snorted with laughter.

"You look like a drowned rat. Oh wow. Hang on, I have to get my phone."

Reuben and Kitty sniggered, and even Jack looked as though he was trying not to laugh.

"Stop it, Sam," Uncle Pete said. "Lucy, are you all right? You didn't hit anything when you fell?"

"No," Lucy muttered. She wasn't hurt, just horribly, horribly embarrassed.

"Never mind," Auntie Cass said. "At least it's a lovely day. It's not really any different to swimming in the lake, is it?" Lucy knew she was being nice but she wasn't helping. It *was* different. No one else had fallen in, and there was water streaming off her. She must look so stupid. Another family was over by the office renting out canoes and they'd probably seen and were laughing at her too...

"Can we go, please?" she said tightly, struggling with the zip on the front of her buoyancy aid. Her fingers were cold and they kept slipping, and in the end Auntie Cass had to do it for her while Lucy stood there and hated everybody.

Lucy had wanted to change out of her wet things but all the clothes had been packed up and the bags were in the trunk of the car. It wasn't a long way back to the house, Auntie Cass said, and she found Lucy a towel to wrap over her damp clothes for the journey. Lucy was trying to pretend she didn't care about falling in but she had a feeling that Auntie Cass and Kitty knew perfectly well how embarrassed she was.

"Lucy, why don't you run in and get a shower and change?" Auntie Cass said kindly as they drew up in front of the house. "We can unload the car. You've been so good sitting there in your wet things and not making a fuss."

Lucy nodded and carefully didn't look at Kitty in case her cousin was laughing at her. Oh, it wasn't fair! When Auntie Cass unlocked the door, she dashed upstairs to get out of her wet clothes.

The hot shower made her feel a lot less grumpy – maybe no one was really bothered? Perhaps she could try and tell it to Mum and Dad as a funny story? She got dressed in her favourite jeans and a cosy hoodie, and decided she'd go back downstairs and help with the unpacking. She leaned down to pick up her damp towel and then stopped, gazing out of the window at the dark shape that had caught her eye.

Lucy's cousins' house didn't really have a garden, not the same way her house did, with grass and bushes and a fence around it all. Instead there was a patch of ground around the house with some gravel and big pots of flowers, and a water feature spilling over a huge rock. Then there were trees – the house was practically in the forest.

Right now, there was also a bear. A small, familiar-looking bear.

The bear cub was sniffing thoughtfully at the water feature. As Lucy watched, he put his tongue out and gave it a tentative lick, as if he wasn't convinced it was really water.

Perhaps it tasted weird from being cycled round the fountain? Lucy laughed softly to herself as the bear stood up on his hind paws and patted at the little bubbling knot of water.

The thing was, she was almost sure it was
the same cub. She could see his chest, as
he reached up to slap his paws at the water
feature, and he had that same little dot of
white, just in the middle where someone would
wear a necklace. Kitty and Martha had said
that bears walked a really long way looking for
food, and it wasn't that far to the campsite by
the lake. It could be the same bear, couldn't it?

But what was he doing, wandering so close
to houses? And where was his mother? What
if he got into trouble and scared someone?
She remembered Kitty and Martha, looking
so solemn and sad as they explained about
wildlife protection officers having to shoot
bears sometimes. Lucy's heart was thudding
again and this time she was frightened for the
bear, not for herself.

Someone shouted something downstairs and Lucy jumped. She needed to tell everyone. What if one of her cousins went out round the back of the house and spooked him?

Lucy gave the cub one last anxious look and raced downstairs.

"Lucy, are you feeling better?" Uncle Pete smiled at her. He was unpacking the canister and putting things back into the fridge.

"Yes – but there's a bear at the back of the house!" Lucy gasped.

"What?" Uncle Pete frowned as though she couldn't have said what he thought she had.

"A bear cub. He's trying to drink out of your rock with the water!"

Everyone else stared at her for a moment, and then plunged out of the kitchen part of the house towards the big windows that looked out over the garden.

Lucy went with them. The bear cub was
so sweet, even if she was anxious about him.
She pressed up against the glass next to Kitty,
wishing that Mum and Dad were here too –
they'd be so disappointed to miss bald eagles
and bears!

There was no bear.

"He's gone…" Lucy said. She supposed she
ought to be pleased – the cub had disappeared
quietly back into the forest, without any kind
of trouble. But it had been so brilliant to see
him playing with the water – he'd seemed to
be having fun. When she'd seen him by the
lake shore, Lucy had been convinced he was
lost, that something had been wrong. He'd
looked so worried. He'd seemed a lot more
relaxed there in the garden.

Perhaps he was just frightened of me?

It felt like a sharp jolt to her heart. But that was probably it, Lucy realized sadly. The cub might not ever have seen people before. He must have been terrified. From everything Kitty and Martha had said about bears getting too close to people, he was right to be – and that felt so sad.

Keep going back into the forest, she thought, gazing at the tall trees outside the house. *There's nothing good here to eat. Stay safe.*

"Huh. Good joke, Lucy. You had us." Sam nodded at her but he didn't sound as though he'd really thought it was funny. Uncle Pete didn't look very amused either.

"It – it's not a joke," Lucy stammered. "He was there. I promise. I didn't make it up. Why would I?"

"Because you were upset about falling in the lake. You didn't like us laughing and you wanted to play a joke on everyone," Sam said, with a shrug.

"I didn't!" Lucy yelled back, suddenly angry. "I didn't make it up and I'm not trying to play a joke. He was there, I'm not lying!"

"Hey, everyone calm down!" Auntie Cass put her hands on Lucy's shoulders. Lucy hadn't noticed that she was shaking until Auntie Cass touched her. "Lucy, no one's cross with you…"

"No one should be, since I haven't done anything!" Lucy pulled away and grabbed Jack's arm. "Do *you* believe me?"

Jack looked at her uncertainly, and then glanced at Reuben and Sam. He really didn't want to get on the wrong side of them, Lucy realized. She was starting to feel a bit sick. Even if Jack did believe her, he didn't want to say so. And besides, she was his little sister – she'd made up stories to tease him or try to show off before. Didn't everyone? But now she was telling the truth and Jack wasn't going to say he believed her.

"I know you didn't like us all seeing you fall in," he muttered, looking down at his feet instead of at her. "But you don't have to make things up just to impress us. It wasn't anything to get upset about – everyone falls in doing that sort of stuff."

Lucy looked round at her aunt and uncle and cousins, all of them staring at her. They all thought she'd made the bear up as a silly joke.

She whirled round and raced back upstairs, flinging herself on to the spare bed set up in Kitty's room. She didn't even have anywhere safe and private to go to be angry, she thought miserably. It was so unfair.

Mum and Dad got back from their trip to the city soon after. Jack and her cousins were all watching a film together downstairs – Lucy thought Auntie Cass might have told them to leave her alone and give her a chance to calm down. Uncle Pete and Auntie Cass were going to have to explain why Lucy was huddled away in Kitty's room. She crept out on to the stairs and sat near the top, trying to listen.

"A bear?" Mum said, her voice somehow sounding high and heavy at the same time. "On her own?"

"Only for about thirty seconds before we caught up with her," Uncle Pete said. "I'm really sorry."

"Not your fault," Dad said, although he sounded strained too. "You explained to them that they mustn't wander off."

"Yeah, but I forgot that Lucy and Jack just don't know it in the same way our kids do. I should have kept more of an eye on her."

"We shouldn't have gone off and left them with you," Mum said and Lucy felt tears stinging at the back of her eyes. Mum and Dad had wanted a night away together – it was supposed to have been their special treat and now she'd ruined it. She hadn't meant to do anything wrong – somehow it had all just happened. Quietly, she eased herself up and padded back into Kitty's room. She hated to think she was spoiling things for Mum and Dad – she knew how excited Dad had been about this trip. It was a once-in-a-lifetime, he'd kept on saying that. She had to try harder. When Auntie Cass called up the stairs that it was dinner time, Lucy stuck on a smile, marched downstairs and offered to help set the table.

"Did Jack tell you about the eagles?" she asked Dad as Uncle Pete served up slices of pizza.

"Eagles?" Mum asked, leaning over the table towards Lucy. She looked anxious. As if she was imagining an eagle swooping down and trying to carry Lucy off, after she'd nearly been eaten by a bear...

"They were amazing!" Lucy said, trying to sound excited and happy and not at all like she'd nearly caused a massive family bust-up. "Bald eagles! We saw them fishing. And did you know they aren't even bald at all?"

Dad gave her a slightly concerned look. Maybe she'd gone a bit far with sounding excited. Or perhaps Uncle Pete had told him she'd made up a story about a bear in the garden. Lucy swallowed hard.

"They were so cool," Jack put in. "You'd have loved them, Dad. The way they just snatched fish out of the water!"

Lucy shot him a grateful look. "And they've got massive great talons!"

"I wish we'd seen them," Dad sighed – and he looked relieved.

"There are lots of different hiking trails that take in the lake," Auntie Cass put in. "Some really amazing places. Pete, why don't we take them to the forest giants? We don't have a plan for tomorrow."

"I love that trail." Uncle Pete nodded eagerly. "The biggest trees you've ever seen. They're cedars. Some of the largest trees in the world, they're incredible to look at."

"I'd love to see them! And eagles would be amazing too," Mum agreed. "Although… Um, no. Don't worry about it. Let's go there tomorrow."

Mum had been going to say something about bears, Lucy was sure. She took a bite of her pizza and chewed it slowly, thinking. Tomorrow she was going to be perfect. She was going to stick to the rest of the hiking party like glue. Nothing was going to ruin this special family trip.

Lucy stood clutching Dad's arm, watching as the eagles wheeled high above them. Their swirling flight pulled at something deep inside her – they looked so right, as though they were exactly where they were meant to be.

"Aren't they amazing?" she whispered to Dad.

"Yes, incredible. I'm so glad we came." Dad slipped his arm round Lucy and squeezed her tight.

"We should get going," Auntie Cass said, looking at her watch. "We don't want to be out too late and, believe me, you'll want to spend time looking at the trees.

I have to hug them every time we hike this trail."

Auntie Cass didn't want them out too late because bears and other wildlife were more active around dawn and dusk, Lucy realized. She wanted to get them safely home again in good time.

"Uh-huh." Uncle Pete looked around. "Everyone OK? We're going to head along the shore a little way and then the trail leads back into the forest."

About ten minutes later, they turned along a narrow path through the trees, and Lucy glanced around curiously. The undergrowth was denser and greener here than anything they'd seen before, and the trees were draped in thick clumps of moss. The path was so quiet it felt as if they were walking into a fairy tale – she almost expected Red Riding Hood to appear, or a wolf. Though she was pretty sure no one had mentioned wolves around here, so perhaps it would be the three bears instead…

"Don't forget to keep talking," Uncle Pete called back, obviously noticing the strange hush. "I'm warning you all, talk or I will sing…"

"I just keep waiting for a dinosaur to look round one of these trees," Dad said. "It feels like the land before time here."

"Dad…" Jack rolled his eyes but Lucy knew exactly what her dad meant.

"Just wait," Uncle Pete said, grinning. "Not long now." He sped up a bit, hurrying them along the path. "There, look."

They'd been walking among tall trees all the way but now there were massive trunks scattered among the younger, thinner ones. They were so gnarled and lumpy that they looked like something out of a cartoon where the trees come to life. Somehow they weren't frightening, though. They looked ancient and wild and wonderful.

"I know what you mean about wanting to hug them," Lucy told Auntie Cass shyly. "They're amazing."

"Right? I'm so glad it's not just me." Auntie Cass beamed at her. "I reckon it would take all of us to hug this one." She pulled Lucy over to the largest tree, which was half hollow at the bottom like a wild, living cave, and they reached out together to stretch as far round the tree as they could. Mum joined on Auntie Cass's other side, but they were still only reaching a tiny part of the massive trunk.

"Kitty! Come and hug the tree with us!"
Auntie Cass called but Kitty didn't seem to hear
her and she disappeared round the other side of
the huge tree chasing Reuben and Sam instead.

"There's an echo!" Mum said, her eyes widening. "From inside the hollow bit, did you hear?"

"Yeah…It's amazing." Lucy leaned against the trunk, resting her cheek against the furrowed bark and wondered how long this tree had been standing here. It was so strange to imagine everything it had lived through. She stayed quiet as they walked on – she didn't feel like singing or chatting and she reckoned the rest of the group was making enough noise.

"What's the matter with you?" Kitty caught up with her.

"Nothing." Lucy shrugged. "I was just thinking about the trees. I can't believe how old they are."

Kitty scowled. "You sound like Mom."

"Hey! Jack, watch out!" There was a yell from

up in front and Lucy gasped as she saw her brother huddled at the base of a huge rock. Reuben and Sam were standing on top of it, looking down, and they glanced guiltily back at the adults.

"Jack, are you OK?" Dad helped him up gently.

"Yeah … but I cut my knee." Jack looked down at his leg and swallowed hard. He wasn't very good with blood, especially if it was his, and his knee was oozing.

"Here." Uncle Pete took off his backpack. "I've got a first-aid kit. It doesn't look deep."

Reuben and Sam scrambled down from the rock, trying not to look as though they'd led Jack up it in the first place. Everyone was fussing but Jack didn't look too bad, Lucy reckoned. It was OK. She sat down on a fallen tree close by and got out her water bottle.

"He shouldn't have been climbing that," Kitty said crossly, slumping down beside her. "Now we're gonna have to wait around for ages."

Lucy looked at her in surprise and Kitty went red with embarrassment. But then she glared back as though Lucy was the one who'd been mean.

"What's the matter?" Lucy asked. "What are you being like that for?"

"I'm not being like anything!" Kitty hissed at her. "Your stupid brother's messing up our hike! After you messed up everything when we went camping!"

Lucy's eyes widened and she gulped. Was that really how Kitty felt? She knew her cousin had been cross with her but she'd thought it was all OK now.

"I wish you guys hadn't come here," Kitty

snapped. And then she jumped up from the
fallen tree and plunged away down a narrow
side path – hardly more than a gap in the ferns.

"Kitty!" Lucy called after her, shocked. Kitty
knew they weren't supposed to leave the group
and go off on their own. It was what she'd just
been telling Lucy off for! "Kitty, come back!"

No one else seemed to notice that Kitty
had gone, they were all still patching up Jack.

THE LOST BEAR CUB

Lucy looked down the little path – she could just see Kitty in her pink top, disappearing round a huge clump of ferns.

Lucy wasn't sure what she'd done to upset her cousin, but she really, *really* didn't want any more family arguments. She'd promised herself that Mum and Dad would get to have a good day.

She shoved her water bottle back in her bag and hared off down the path to fetch Kitty before anyone else realized she wasn't there.

"Kitty! Kitty! Where are you? Come back!"
Lucy hissed. She glanced back along the
little path, checking to see if anyone had
spotted she'd gone. But all the family were still
gathered round Jack. Lucy hurried on. There
was an enormous tree up ahead and Lucy was
sure she could see her cousin's pink T-shirt just
beyond it.

"Kitty! Stop messing about!" she called,
darting round the tree and expecting to see
her cousin – maybe Kitty was hiding behind it,
waiting to jump out at her. Then she stopped,

looking at the empty clearing and feeling foolish. There was no sign of Kitty anywhere. A bird whistled in the branches high above her and there was a quiet rustling among the bushes, but that was all. Certainly no cousin waiting to tease her.

Where had Kitty gone? Feeling cross now, Lucy stomped round the tree, looking for different paths she might have taken. The problem was, there seemed to be little paths everywhere, narrow tracks weaving in and out of the bushes or under branches. Lucy started down what seemed the most likely one but then it faded away to nothing after a few metres.

The bird chattered again above her head, making her jump. Lucy felt suddenly scared. She was almost sure there was someone there, watching her. She could feel the eyes prickling her skin. "Kitty?" she whispered, but no one answered.

In a panic, Lucy plunged on through the bushes, feeling them catch and tear at her leggings. Another bird fluttered out of the undergrowth in front of her, making her squeak with fear – and then she broke out on to the path again, a wider one that had wooden planks set into the muddy ground to make it easier to walk on. Lucy caught her breath, resting her hands on her knees and letting the weird dizzy panic die away. For a moment, she'd felt as if she was completely alone and abandoned – the only human among all these ancient trees. But that couldn't be true, not when someone had built a path.

She stood up slowly and looked around. Still no sign of Kitty. And what was worse, after her wild dash through the bushes, Lucy had lost her bearings entirely. She had no idea how to get back to the rest of the family. She'd set off down the path to rescue Kitty but now she was completely lost too. *Maybe even more lost than Kitty,* she admitted to herself. Her cousin had done this hike before – she might know exactly where she was heading.

"She still shouldn't have gone off on her own," Lucy whispered to herself. "We're supposed to stay with everyone else. That's why *she* was so cross with *me!*"

And now she was on her own all over again, just as she had been at the lake. There could be hundreds of bears peacefully minding their own business in this ancient forest.

Perhaps she hadn't imagined those eyes she'd been sure were watching her.

"Kitty!" Lucy yelled. She wasn't actually calling for Kitty – she just needed to make a noise so all those bears kept out of her way, and talking to herself was too lonely and strange. "Kitty, come on! I'm sorry I messed up the lake trip! I never meant to. Jack's going to be fine in a minute, we can keep going with the hike! Just come back! Please!"

"OK, OK. You don't need to go on about it."

Lucy screamed. She'd been so busy shouting, she hadn't even heard Kitty walking up behind her. Then she threw her arms round her cousin and hugged her hard. "I found you!"

"I found you, actually." But Kitty hugged her back. "I didn't mean for you to come after me," she said, looking embarrassed.

"Are you OK?"

Kitty shrugged. "Yeah."

"But you ran off – you were so upset."

Kitty stirred the brownish leaf litter with
the toe of her hiking boot and sighed. "I was
jealous."

Lucy blinked. "Jealous? Of me? What for? I kept messing everything up. You were all laughing at me!"

"But nobody minded you doing things wrong, because you're the littlest!" Kitty protested. "Everybody kept making excuses for you. My dad was all, *She doesn't understand, you can't get annoyed with her wandering off, it's not her fault.* And my mom was fussing over you all the time." Kitty lifted one shoulder in a grumpy half-shrug. "*Lucy's so cute and polite. Lucy has such sweet manners. You have to look after Lucy, she's younger than you.* Just because you like hugging trees," she muttered.

"Oh…" Lucy stared at her cousin. She hadn't picked up on *any* of that. She'd just about noticed that Kitty didn't want to join in hugging the massive tree but that was all.

"I thought you liked that I was younger than you," she said, her voice very small. "You kept telling me that you were older and I didn't know anything."

Kitty sighed. "Yeah. I know. No one said it made sense… I guess I'm just used to Mom fussing over *me* and telling Reuben and Sam they have to look after their little sister."

Lucy nodded. She knew she got away with more stuff than Jack did – he was always telling her how unfair it was.

"And then you were there and suddenly I wasn't the youngest any more. Even though I used to complain about it all the time, I did kinda like it." She nudged Lucy with her elbow. "You came looking for me. Even though my dad told you off the other day when we were at the lake."

"I suppose I should have just told your mum and dad you'd gone – but I didn't want everyone getting upset… I thought I could get you back before anyone noticed." Lucy looked around at the trees and sighed. "We're lost, aren't we?"

Kitty moved a step closer to her and shivered. "Yeah. But – but I reckon if we keep shouting really loud, they'll hear us. We didn't go all that far. Did we?"

"I don't think so. You don't know any of the wilderness stuff that your dad kept telling us about? Like, which side of the tree moss grows on?"

"Oh, I know *that*." Kitty brightened up for a moment and there was a flash of the big cousin about her again. "North. In the northern hemisphere. But Dad said moss grows just about anywhere it wants to. It doesn't matter anyway. We could probably find north by looking at the moss or looking at the stars if we waited till night-time – but we don't know which direction we came in, so it wouldn't help."

"Oh. I see what you mean." Lucy looked up the wooden path. "We could follow this? I mean, it's a bigger path, isn't it? Maybe it leads to a road and we could find somebody and borrow a phone?"

Kitty frowned. "I guess. But what if we're just heading in the wrong direction, away from everyone else?"

"I was by one of those huge trees," Lucy said thoughtfully. "Then I got spooked because it felt like someone was watching me, and I ran… I'm pretty sure I came straight out on to the path – so if we go back here – yes, look!

You can see where I trod on these plants!"
She showed Kitty the crushed undergrowth.
"And here as well." She grabbed Kitty's hand
and towed her forwards through the bushes.
"We're looking for a big tree."

Kitty snorted. "Like there's only one of those around here." But then she added, "Sorry. You're doing great. I should have paid more attention to where I was going, I was just too mad to think."

Lucy squeezed her cousin's hand and then pointed ahead. "There, I was right! I'm sure it was that tree." She sped up, pulling Kitty harder, and walked around the huge tree trunk, nodding. "It was definitely this one. I remember that branch. It's like a hand."

Kitty nodded. "OK. We're definitely closer then."

"Yeah, but now I'm not sure how I got here. I couldn't work out which path you'd taken so I went looking all round and I lost which way we'd come. Then something spooked me, it was weird. I was sure someone was watching me."

Lucy glanced up at the tree and then her fingers bit into Kitty's palm.

"Hey, don't do that, it hurts!"

"Kitty, look!" Lucy whispered shakily.

"OK, but let go of me…" Kitty followed Lucy's gaze up into the tree and her complaints died away. Stretched out along one of the branches, staring down at them, was a huge yellow-brown cat – like a leopard but without any spots.

"What is it?" Lucy asked, as the cat began to stand up.

"A cougar, I think. Lucy, we have to back away. Uh – try and look big. We have to look like too much trouble to hunt." Kitty stepped back slowly and Lucy went with her. Part of her brain was saying how beautiful the cat was – its eyes were a clear gold colour, darkly rimmed in black. It didn't look that different to Shadow or Lucy's cat Billy in some ways. The same neat pink nose and puffy white muzzle, dotted with whiskers.

We're a lot too close if I can see its whiskers… the more awake part of Lucy said, and she moved back a little faster.

"Don't run," Kitty said and then her voice shook as she added, "If we run, it'll think it ought to chase us."

But the cougar was slipping down from the tree branch now, moving so gracefully that it seemed to flow. It landed on the ground and paced towards the girls, breathing a low growl.

"Go away!" Kitty yelled. "Bad cat! No!" and Lucy joined in. "Get away!"

The cougar stopped, looking uncertainly between the two girls. It spat at them – the

same way Lucy had seen Billy spit at a dog
that dared to walk past their front garden.

Kitty ducked down for a second, grabbing
a stick from the ground, and threw it at the
cougar. The huge cat batted it away and the
growling rose to a strange, terrifying yowl.

THE LOST BEAR CUB

It showed a mouthful of dagger-sharp teeth but it was looking sideways now – as if it was trying to work out an escape route.

"Come back a bit more," Lucy said, pulling at Kitty. "It can't get past us. I think it wants to go, but it's stuck between us and the tree."

They edged back again, feeling cautiously behind them at each step – the cougar was a little quieter now, the angry growls giving way to a softer hissing.

And then Kitty stumbled, falling down on to one knee, and the cougar leaped.

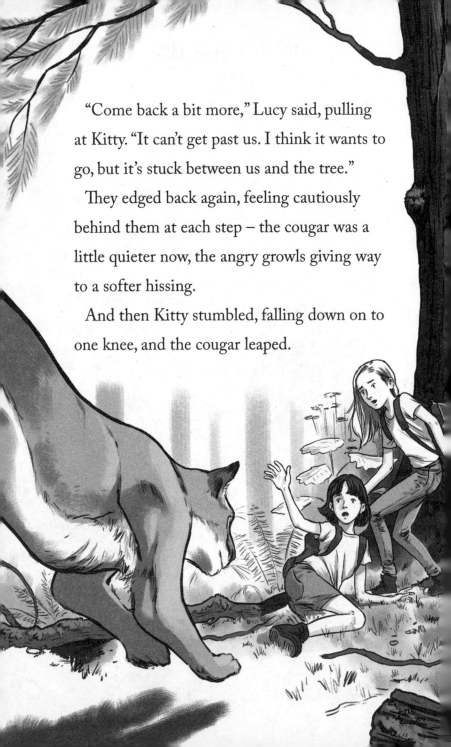

The cougar sprang forwards, slapping its heavy paws on the ground and growling louder than ever. Lucy was convinced it was about to leap on them – she dragged Kitty back, hauling her cousin along the ground until she could stagger upright – but the cougar stayed a couple of metres away, still snarling furiously and pawing at the earth.

"Are you OK?" Lucy gasped, holding Kitty tight. "Are you hurt?" And then she yelled at the cougar, "Leave her alone! Get away! Just go away! We don't want to hurt you, just go!"

The cat twisted, hissing, and then made an angry rush forwards again – but this time, not at the two girls. Instead, it darted at a patch of thick undergrowth, off to the side of the tiny clearing round the tree.

Lucy and Kitty took the chance to stumble back a few more steps. Lucy wanted to turn and run as fast as they could but Kitty had said running was a bad idea – it would make them look like prey.

"What's it looking at?" she whispered to Kitty. "Is there something hiding in those bushes?"

"There must be," Kitty agreed.

The cougar snarled and clawed at whatever was in the bushes – but then it jumped back uncertainly, with an angry yowl. What could be big enough to surprise a cougar?

Then out of the undergrowth barrelled an angry bear – a black bear, making a strange hooting noise low in her throat and swiping at the cougar with massive paws.

"She's got a cub with her," Lucy gasped, seeing a smaller bear peer worriedly out of the bushes at the furious cat.

The bear swung her head, looking back at her cub, and he dashed out from behind her with a yelp, shooting across the little clearing to a tall pine tree. The girls watched, amazed, as he hugged the trunk and clambered up, incredibly fast. He stopped about halfway up the tree, settling on a thick branch and peering down on the fight.

"She sent him up there out of the way," Kitty whispered. "She didn't want him anywhere near that cougar."

The cougar was still growling furiously and
swiping at the mother bear, but it was definitely
retreating. The bear kept lumbering up on
to her hind legs, which made her look huge.

Lucy couldn't tell if she was doing it on
purpose to be scary or if she just wanted to get
a better view of what was going on, but she was
terrifyingly tall and the cougar seemed to think
so too. It was backed up almost to the massive
cedar tree now – it hardly had anywhere left
to go. Then it slashed its paws at the bear one
last time and turned tail, slinking away and
disappearing into the low bushes on the far side
of the clearing.

The bear snorted and shook herself, then
glanced round at Kitty and Lucy, who were
standing among the ferns, still watching her.
She eyed them for a moment, and then walked
over to the tall pine tree where the cub was
watching. She grunted softly – which must
have meant that he was to come down, as he
started to wriggle along his branch at once.

He came back down the slim tree trunk
bottom first, and Lucy wanted to laugh. She
knew she shouldn't, they were still much, much
too close to an unpredictable wild bear who
was frightened for her baby. But the little cub
was so funny – and the bears were a lot less
scary than the cougar had been. She felt like
she almost *knew* the bears now.

The cub arrived on the ground in a rush and
a jump and nuzzled at his mother. Then he
looked round curiously at Lucy and Kitty.

"That's the same bear cub we saw at the
lake…" Kitty murmured. She sounded as
though she didn't want to believe it. "He's got
a white spot on his chest, I saw it then…"

Lucy nodded at her. "Yes! And I did see him
in your garden too, you know. I didn't make
it up. It's been the same cub every time."

She frowned worriedly. "Do you think he's getting too used to people? Does he recognize us? Maybe we ought to shout at him or something, to try and scare him away. I'd hate it if we made him start coming closer to hikers and someone reported him as dangerous."

"She's looking at us," Kitty said worriedly.

The mother bear was gazing at them thoughtfully. She snuffed the air a few times, and then set off across the clearing, shooing the cub along with her. But when she reached a narrow little track through the tall ferns and bushes, she stopped. Looking back at the two girls, she grunted again, the same way she had to her cub. Almost as if she was telling them to hurry up and follow her.

"Do you think…?" Lucy began hesitantly.

Kitty nodded. "She's waiting for us, isn't she?

She chased away the cougar, and now she's looking out for us."

Slowly, the two girls stepped forwards, just one little step at a time – ready to jump back again if the bear showed any sign of fear or anger. But she didn't. She set off through the bushes again, looking back every so often to make sure her two strange charges were following along.

"We don't even know if she's taking us the right way!" Kitty whispered – but she didn't stop following.

"I bet she is. She's clever. She probably knows exactly where all the hikers in her bit of forest are," Lucy said. "Hey! Listen, did you hear that?"

"Kitty! Lucy!" It was very faint, somewhere off in the distance ahead of the bear. The bear looked round at them again, and Lucy wondered if there was a look in her eyes that said, *There, you see?* But she was probably just imagining it.

"That was my dad!" Kitty gasped. "She *is* taking us back to them!"

"And I can see that huge tree, the one your mum was trying to hug." Lucy pointed out excitedly. "That's it, isn't it? I can see the hollow bit."

The mother bear stopped and then drew her cub off to the side, a few metres away from the tiny track through the bushes. She stood there, watching the two girls as another shout echoed through the trees.

"Thank you," Lucy said quietly as she and

Kitty walked along the path. She kept turning back to look at the bears – partly to make sure that they weren't following, but mostly because it felt like they were saying goodbye. She wanted to wave. She did, just a tiny wave so that Kitty wouldn't see her and laugh.

The cub was leaning round his mother's legs to see them better and Lucy smiled at him and whispered, "Bye, bear…"

Kitty was a little ahead now, calling, "Mom! Dad! We're here!" and Lucy turned back and hurried after her.

"You're here! Hey, I've got them!" Uncle Pete grabbed Kitty and swung her up into a hug. "Where have you been?"

"Did you see the cougar?" Jack yelled, running at Lucy and grabbing her hands. His knee had a big white dressing on it but he didn't seem to be limping. "Are you OK? There was this great big cat!"

Mum and Dad were right behind him, hugging her all over. Mum kept saying, "What happened?" and "Oh, Lucy!" and "We were so worried."

Kitty and Lucy exchanged a glance. How much should they say? Was it better just to keep quiet and not worry everyone?

But Auntie Cass was holding Kitty at arm's length now, looking her up and down. "You're covered in dirt – what happened, did you fall? Are you hurt? Kitty, talk to me!"

"I'm fine, Mom!"

"Where did you girls go? What were you thinking?" Auntie Cass demanded.

Kitty sighed, a huge sigh that made her shoulders heave. "I was upset and I ran off, and Lucy came to find me."

"But – but you know how dangerous that is!" Uncle Pete looked as though he didn't understand. "We've just seen a cougar – it could have attacked you."

"It's OK," Lucy said, seeing her mum's stricken face. Mum was imagining what might have happened and Lucy hated it. "It didn't hurt us. Mum, don't worry. Kitty fell over when the cougar came at us but the bear chased it off. We were fine."

Kitty rolled her eyes sideways and Lucy realized she hadn't explained that in the most reassuring way.

"The cougar came at you?" Auntie Cass whispered. "There was a *bear*?"

"The same bear cub Lucy saw at the lake. And at the house," Kitty explained. "They looked out for us, Mom. The mother bear totally scared off the cougar and then she showed us the path to get back to you. I promise."

"She really was looking after us." Lucy nodded. "I don't know if the cougar was going to attack – I think maybe it just wanted to get away, but it got angry when it knew we'd spotted it. It was up in this big cedar tree." She shivered and turned to her cousin, her eyes widening. "Kitty, I was right! When I thought someone was watching me, there was! It was the cougar all the time!"

Dad swallowed hard and pulled Lucy close to him on one side and Jack on the other. "I think we should get moving."

Uncle Pete nodded, taking Kitty's hand in his. "Yeah, I'm feeling like we need some walls between us and the wildlife right now."

As they headed on along the trail, Lucy could hear the faint sound of the waves from the lake hitting the shore and birds calling to each other high above. She glanced back behind them, wanting a last glimpse of that massive cedar tree – and her breath caught in her throat as she saw a small black bear watching her, peeping out of the hollow in the trunk.

"Stay safe," Lucy whispered. "Goodbye!"

She had to hope she'd never see him again. That he'd head off deep into the wilder parts of the forest and live his happy bear life far from people. But it was so hard to walk away from him and his mother, and know that she was seeing them for the last time.

The bear cub padded off round the tree trunk and Lucy turned away, leaning against her dad as they walked along the trail. A gleam of sun was falling through the trees, splashing the path ahead with shadows. Even though Lucy was still shaky with from their cougar encounter, she felt deep down that they'd been so lucky. The bears had been there just at the perfect time to protect her and Kitty. It was as if this ancient forest had known they needed help. Lucy ran her hand over the deep, ridged bark of a massive cedar tree and smiled. "Thank you…"

Read an extract from

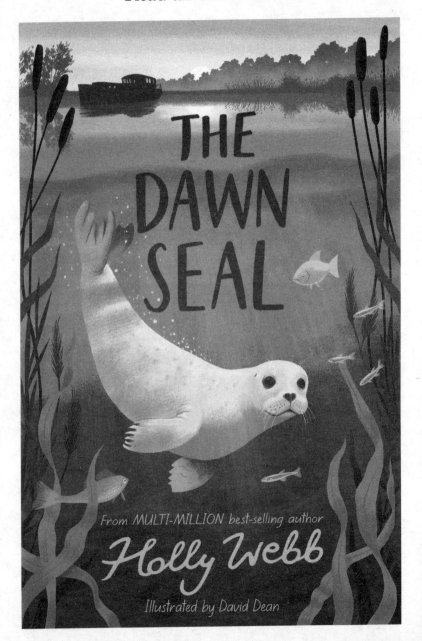

THE
DAWN
SEAL

From MULTI-MILLION best-selling author

Holly Webb

Illustrated by David Dean

"Oh, Dad! It's beautiful!" Lissa stood on the riverbank, looking at the line of boats and the sun glittering on the water.

Dad grinned at her. "Good, isn't it? Even if it is a pain having to carry everything along the path." He hefted Lissa's huge backpack further up on to his shoulder. "How much stuff did you bring, Liss…"

"I'm here the whole summer!" Lissa pointed out. "I need clothes. And Mum said she wasn't sure how easy it is to do washing on a boat."

"I do have a washing machine," Dad said.

"Everything you'd find in a normal house, actually. Just smaller. But there's not much space inside for hanging anything out to dry."

"Which boat is yours?" Lissa asked eagerly. Dad had sent her photos of his new home, but she was finding it hard to work out which one it was. There were so many boats moored along the riverbank, of all shapes and sizes. One of them looked like a battleship, only smaller. And there was even one with a tall mast and furled sails. Lissa had never thought she'd see huge sailing ships on the river.

It seemed so strange that her dad was actually living here now. The river was about as different from Lissa's street back home as she could imagine.

At first, she'd thought it was going to be weird spending her summer holidays with Dad on a barge, but now she was realizing just how exciting it could be. Still … she wished Mum was here to see the beautiful boats too. And Zoe. Zoe would love them – except she'd be bouncing around all over the place and Mum and her partner Mickey would be panicking about her falling in the river. *It probably wouldn't be a good idea to have a two-year-old on a boat,* Lissa thought.

Dad smiled. "Over there. She's called *Rose Dawn,* can you see her? The name's painted on the front."

"She?" Lissa frowned.

"All boats are called she," Dad explained. "It's traditional, I think. Even if they're called something like, I don't know, *Trevor.* Still a she."

"That's weird… Oh yes! I can see her. The blue one? Dad, she's huge!"

"What, did you think you were going to spend the summer living on a tiny rowing boat?" Dad was laughing but he sounded proud.

He loves the boat already, Lissa thought, and something tugged inside her. *Rose Dawn* was Dad's home – but perhaps that meant Lissa could belong here on the river too?

Lissa's parents had split up a few years before, but Dad had always been close by and Lissa had been able to see him almost every day, even though she was living with her mum. Now Dad had moved to this houseboat on the river, an hour's drive away. He'd explained it was something he'd wanted to do for a long time – and it would be good for him to be closer to London for work. He'd promised that they'd still see each other as much as before – more even, because Lissa would come and stay and it would be special.

But Lissa wasn't convinced, even though Dad kept saying how exciting it would be to stay with him on a boat. How could she spend as much time with her dad when she couldn't just run round the corner and knock on the door of his flat? Already she hadn't seen him for over a month, while he'd been moving in and sorting out everything on the boat… When he'd arrived to pick her up, he'd looked almost strange. It was just for a moment, while Lissa got used to his hair being longer, but it had been a bit of a shock.

Still. They were going to make up for lost time now.

"*Rose Dawn*'s a Dutch barge." Dad interrupted Lissa's thoughts, still sounding so pleased and proud. "A long time ago they were built of wood, and they were sailing boats that carried cargo around the canals in Holland. But most of the newer ones like *Rose Dawn* are metal, and they have engines instead of sails. Although she's nearly a hundred years old, so not that new!"

Dad set off down the path along the side of the river and Lissa hurried after him. A couple of the boats they passed had people sitting out on the little decks at each end, and one man was sunbathing in a chair on the path – they all waved at her and Dad, and Lissa smiled shyly back.

"Are they your neighbours?" she whispered to Dad. "Does everyone stay here all the time, or do the boats move?"

"A bit of both," Dad explained. "*Rose Dawn* has an engine, so I can move her, but I've paid for the spot where she's moored. It's a bit like renting a house, I suppose. But I could take my own house on holiday with me! I'd just set off up the river without having to do any packing. Isn't that brilliant?"

"I suppose…" Lissa agreed a bit doubtfully. She couldn't quite imagine it. Her house belonged in her street – with her friend Grace next door but one, and school just round the corner, and all the dogs and cats she liked to wave to in their different windows. It wasn't just the *house* that was home, it was the place too.

Dad juggled the bags about a bit so he could put his arm round Lissa's shoulders. "Everything's going to be OK, don't worry."

"I'm not worried *really*…"

"It must feel strange though, the thought of being away from your mum the whole summer. But we'll have fun, I promise."

Lissa nodded. She loved spending time with Dad, that wasn't the problem. But he was right, six weeks away from home was a big change.

"Here you go." Dad lifted Lissa's backpack over the side of the boat and then held out a hand to help her climb on board. Lissa stood under a sort of canopy roof and felt the boat shift beneath her feet slightly. There was water underneath her, which made her tummy feel a little odd – but Lissa didn't mind it.

"This bit's called the wheelhouse," Dad said, clambering on behind her and pointing to a polished wooden steering wheel, surrounded by complicated-looking dials and gauges. "And we go down these steps and along here into the saloon." He led Lissa down into a cosy living room, with a sofa built into the side of the boat, and a couple of armchairs. "Then this end is the kitchen – except on a boat you call it the galley."

Also available

Illustrated by Dawn Cooper

THE
WILDMEADOW
HARE

From MULTI-MILLION best-selling author

Holly Webb

Ellie used to love watching the hares leap
and play on the common with her mum.
But since Mum passed away it's getting
harder to remember those happy memories.

Until one day, Ellie finds an injured baby
hare. The poor animal looks so scared,
she has to do something to help. Nursing
the hare back to health will be a big
responsibility, but could it be Ellie's chance
to feel close to her mum again?

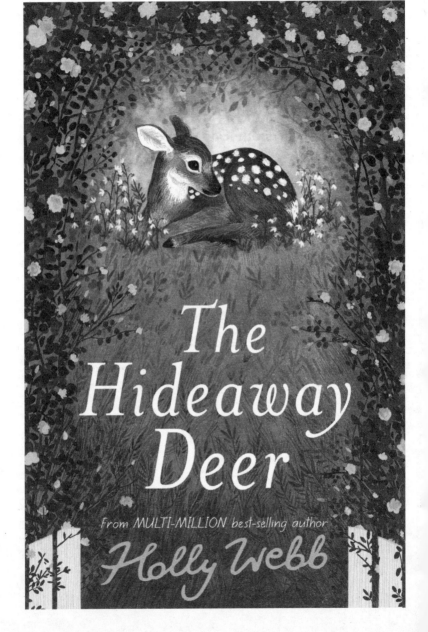

The
Hideaway
Deer

From MULTI-MILLION best-selling author

Holly Webb

When Lola moves house she can't help
worrying about leaving her old life behind.
There are some good things, though.
She loves her home with its huge, rambling
garden and the deer that sometimes wander
in through the broken fence.

Then one day Lola comes across a fawn who
seems to be in trouble. She's determined to do
everything she can to help the terrified little
deer, but will she be able to do it on her own?

HOLLY WEBB

Holly Webb started out as a children's book editor and wrote her first series for the publisher she worked for. She has been writing ever since, with over one hundred and fifty books to her name. Holly lives in Berkshire, with her husband and three children. Holly's pet cats are always nosying around when she is trying to type on her laptop.

For more information about Holly Webb visit:

www.holly-webb.com